Silvanus P. Thompson

William Gilbert, and Terrestrial Magnetism in the Time of Queen Elizabeth: A Discourse

Outlook

Silvanus P. Thompson

William Gilbert, and Terrestrial Magnetism in the Time of Queen Elizabeth: A Discourse

1. Auflage | ISBN: 978-3-73262-992-3

Erscheinungsort: Frankfurt am Main, Deutschland

Erscheinungsjahr: 2018

Outlook Verlag GmbH, Frankfurt.

WILLIAM GILBERT, AND TERRESTRIAL MAGNETISM IN THE TIME OF QUEEN ELIZABETH: A DISCOURSE BY SILVANUS P. THOMPSON, F.R.S.

WILLIAM GILBERT AND TERRESTRIAL MAGNETISM IN THE TIME OF QUEEN ELIZABETH.

WILLIAM GILBERT, the father of electrical science, was born in Colchester in 1540. Educated at St. John's College, Cambridge, where he took his degree as Doctor of Medicine in 1569, he settled, after four years of foreign travel, in London in 1573, and was admitted to the Royal College of Physicians, of which he became Censor, Treasurer, and, in 1599, President. He was in February, 1601, appointed personal Physician to the Queen, whom he attended in her last illness. He came of a well-known East Anglian family, and held extensive landed estates in Essex and Suffolk. He survived the Queen only eight months, dying November 30th, 1603.

GILBERT's monumental work, the *De Magnete*, published in 1600, marks an era in magnetic science. For some four hundred years the employment of the magnetic needle in navigation had been known both in Northern and Southern Europe. While it is possible that the primitive use of the loadstone may be ascribed to the Baltic, it is certain that the employment of a pivotted needle, and the addition of a rose of the winds as a compass card both originated in the Mediterranean. The pivotted needle is described in the Epistle of Peter Peregrinus, written in 1269; while the earliest known compass-card marked with the initials of the names of the winds is that ascribed to Jachobus Giraldis, of 1426, in the Biblioteca Marciana in Venice. The manner of use in Elizabethan times of the loadstone and of the compass may be gathered from Olaus Magnus (*Historia de Gentibus Septentrionalibus*, 1555), from Pedro de

Medina (*Arte de Nauegar*, 1545), Martinus Cortes (*Breve compendio de la sphera*, 1556), Blundevile (*Exercises*, 1594), Norman (*Newe Attractive*, 1581), Borough (*A discours of the Variation of the Cumpas*, 1581), Pedro Nuñez (*Instrumenta Artis Navigandi*, 1592), Barlow (*The Navigators Supply*, 1597), Nautonier (*Mécometrie de l'Eyman*, 1602), and Stevin (*Die Havenvinding*, 1599).

At the time when steering by the compass was introduced into navigation, the compass pointed in Middle Europe so nearly truly to the north that with the rough instrumental appliances at hand its deviation from the true north was seldom noticed, or if noticed ascribed to some error in the setting of the needle. Later the compass-makers began to set their needles slightly askew beneath the card, according to the variation in the place of origin. Norman (1581) states that those used in the Levant, made in Sicily, Genoa, or Venice, had the needles straight, while those used in Denmark and Flanders had them set at three-quarters of a point, or a whole point, to the eastward; while those made in Spain, Portugal, France, and England, had the needles set half a point to the east. Those for Russia were set at "three seconds of a point." Gilbert denounced these devices as tending to obscure the true facts. Gradually it became recognized, probably after the voyage of Columbus, when the manifest change in the declination of the needle nearly caused mutiny of the sailors, that the direction of the needle differs at different places; and accordingly navigators began to collect data. The record of the voyage of Columbus states that during his second voyage in 1496 he used for steering the observations made on the declination during his first voyage. The "secret" of Sebastian Cabot, which he declared when dying to be a divine revelation to him, can have been little else than the idea of using in navigation the local declinations of the compass. On the other hand, Pedro de Medina flatly denied the existence of the declination, adding that if the compass did not show the pole, the fault lay in the defective construction of the compass itself. Columbus had found a point $2\frac{1}{2}°$ east of Corvo, in the Azores, where there was "no variation," and other navigators explored the "agonic" lines which crossed the Atlantic and the Indian ocean. According to Humboldt, Alonzo de Santa Cruz in 1530 constructed the first general variation chart. But along with this development of practical interest in the subject there grew up a crop of wild legends to account for the irregularities observed. The reason why the compass needle pointed north, and the reason why it did not point truly north, were alike proclaimed to be due to the stars, to the influence of spirits, or to the existence of loadstone mountains of uncertain locality and of fabulous power. The old traditions of the Arabian Nights, dressed in a newer setting, found themselves justified by the insertion in maps of loadstone rocks, the position of which changed at the fancy of the chartographer. Ptolemy had located them in the Manioles; Olaus Magnus declared them to be under the pole; Garzias ab Horto situated them in the region of Calcutta. The map of Johann Ruysch, which adorned the edition of Ptolemy, publisht at Rome in 1508, showed four magnetic islands in the Arctic Circle. Martinus Cortes placed the loadstone mountains in Sarmatia. Mercator in his great chart depicted two great rocks rising from the sea to the north of eastern Siberia, one being drawn on the supposition that at St. Michael the compass points due north, while the other is further north on the supposition that the compass points due north at Corvo. The map of Cornelius Wytfliet, 1597, shows the same phantom islands. Blundevile, writing in 1594 of the now lost map of Peter Plancius, mentions that he sets down the pole of the loadstone somewhat to southward of the islands that lie east of Groynelande.

Meantime another significant fact had been discovered in 1576 by Robert Norman, of Limehouse, compass-maker, namely, the tendency of the magnetized needle to dip its northern end downwards. Noticing this as a circumstance that occasioned him some trouble in the construction of his compasses, he thereupon devised a dipping-needle, and measured the dip, "which for this Cyty of London I finde by exact obseruations to be about 71 degrees 50 mynutes." He attributed both the declination and the dip of the needle to the existence of a "poynt respective," which the needle respected or indicated, but toward which it was not attracted. The first authoritative treatise on the variation of the compass was the tract by William Borough, comptroller to the Navy, who in 1580 found an eastward declination of 11° 15' at Limehouse. Borough had himself travelled in northern regions and had found at Vaigats a westerly declination of 7 degrees, whereas by Norman's theory of the respective point there should have been an easterly declination of 49° 22'. The great navigators were continually bringing home fresh information. Drake, Lynschoten, Cavendish, Hariot all contributed; as did lesser men such as Abraham Kendall, sailing- master to Sir Robert Dudley (the *soi-disant* Duke of Northumberland), and afterward companion of Drake in his last voyage. Teachers of navigation such as Simon Stevin of Bruges and Edward Wright, lecturer to the East India Company, might record and tabulate: but a master-mind was wanting to forge some larger and consistent doctrine which should afford a grasp of the whole subject. Such an one arose in Dr. William Gilbert. Nurtured, as we have seen, in the Cambridge which had so recently been the home of Linacre and of Kaye—the Kaye who founded Caius College— Gilbert had, during his subsequent sojourn in Italy, conversed with all the learned men of his time. He had experimented on the magnet with Fra Paolo Sarpi: he had, there is reason to think, met Giordano Bruno: he was the friend and correspondent of Giovanni Francesco Sagredo. Being a man of means and a bachelor, he spent money freely upon books, maps, instruments, minerals, and magnets. For twenty years he experimented ceaselessly, and read, and wrote and speculated, and tested his speculations by new experiments. For eighteen years he kept beside him the manuscript of his treatise, which in the year 1600 saw the light under the title of *De Magnete*, to which was added the sub-title: *magneticisque corporibus, et de magno magnete tellure, physiologia nova.* That which Gilbert had in fact perceived, and which none before him had glimpsed even dimly, was that the globe of the earth itself acted as a great loadstone, and that the tendency of the needle to point in a polar direction was due to the globe acting as a whole. So he boldly put into his title-page the statement that his new philosophy was concerning the great magnet the earth: and in chapter after chapter he set himself to describe the experiments upon which he founded his famous induction. The phrase *terrestrial magnetism* does not occur in any of the prior treatises, because the idea had not presented itself. Gilbert piled proof upon proof, sometimes most cogently, as when he constructed loadstone globes, or *terrellas* to serve as magnetic models of the earth; sometimes with indifferent logic, as when he pointed to the iron ore in the earth and reasoned that the magnet tended to conform to (*i.e.* turn itself toward) the homogenic substance of the body from which it had been dug. The local deviations of the compass he sought to account for by the irregularities of the earth's crust, and maintained that the compass tended always, at places off the coast of a continent, to be deflected somewhat toward that continent. His syllogism was based on the fact that at that date all the way up the Atlantic seaboard of Europe, from Morocco to Norway, the variation was eastward. He argued that this was a universal law. But even within one generation, as may be seen in *Purchas his Pilgrims*, in the narrative of the voyage of Bylot and Baffin, the generality of the law was questioned. Gilbert reasoned on such knowledge as he had, and this did not include any notion of the secular changes in the declination. In his time, as he tells us, the variation of the compass at London was 11- 1/3 degrees. What he did not know was that this was a diminishing quantity which in fifty-seven years would be reduced to zero, to be succeeded by a westward declination that would last for nearly three hundred years. For the facts as known in the thirty years succeeding Gilbert's death, see the remarkable and scarce volume of Gellibrand: *A Discourse Mathematical on the Variation of the Magneticall Needle* (1635).

Gilbert's treatise is a skilful literary achievement in which there is no trace to reveal whether any part was written before the rest. It is divided systematically into six books. The sixth book only appears to suffer from some incompleteness. It relates not so much to the magnet as to the Copernican theory of the universe, which doctrine Gilbert had eagerly espoused, and which he was the first in England to proclaim. It is known from a letter to Barlow, printed in 1616, that he intended to add to it certain chapters descriptive of some of his instruments, but he had not completed these before his death. The first book treats of historic accounts of the loadstone, of its origin and properties, of iron ores in general, and of the fables and vain opinions which in the handling of Paracelsus and of the schoolmen had grown up around the magnet. The second book is on the magnetic motions, and primarily on the attractions and repulsions between loadstones, between loadstone and iron, and between magnetic needles. In this book occurs the notable digression upon the subject of amber and the electric forces of amber and of other substances which when rubbed show, as he discovered, similar electrical powers. An analysis of this part, and a summary of Gilbert's electrical discoveries will be found in the Notes printed for the Gilbert Club to accompany the English translation (1900) of the *De Magnete*. After this digression Gilbert returns to the attractive properties of the loadstone, and to the way they are affected by giving it different shapes. In the course of this enquiry, he announces his discovery of the augmentation of the power of the loadstone by arming it with iron caps, an invention which caused Galileo to say: "I extremely praise, admire, and envy this author for that a conception so stupendous should come into his mind. I think him moreover worthy of extraordinary applause for the many new and true observations that he has made." Gilbert further pointed out that the loadstone is surrounded by a sort of atmosphere or "orbe of virtue" within which the magnetical effects can be observed. Book 3, on the directive force of the magnet, is full of most instructive experiments, in which the terrella figures largely, relating to the question how one magnet influences another and tends to make it point toward it. All this was leading up to the theory of terrestrial magnetism; for we find him naming the parts of his loadstone globes with poles, equator and meridians. In this book he dilates on the observation that vertical iron rods, such as the finial on the Church of St. John at Rimini, spontaneously acquired magnetic properties. This he traced to the influence of the earth, and demonstrated the effect by magnetizing iron bars by simply hammering them on the anvil while they lay in a north and south position. Book 4 deals with the Declination, or, as it was then called, the variation of the compass. He discusses its observation and measurement, the influence of islands, the results obtained by travellers to distant parts, Nova Zembla, the Guinea coast, the Canary Isles, Florida, Virginia, Cape Race, and Brazil. Then he recounts his experiments with terrellas having uneven surfaces to represent the irregularities of the earth's crust. He points out errors arising from the fallacious practice of setting the needle obliquely under the card. He considers in separate chapters the variations in Nova Zembla, in the Pacific, in the Mediterranean, and in the Eastern Ocean. The fifth book is on the Dip. Gilbert seized with avidity on Norman's discovery of this effect, and devised an improved form of dipping-needle. He experimented on the dip of compass-needles placed at different points over his terrella, and evolved a theory on the proportion which he conceived to exist between the latitude and the dip. Arguing from all too imperfect data, he propounded the view that the dip was the same in any given latitude; and proposed that seamen should ascertain their latitudes by simply observing the dip. He was aware that local irregularities might occur, as they do in the declination; but was not deterred by this knowledge from propounding his theory with much circumstance and considerable geometrical skill. After the publication of his book he developed the theory still further and gave it to Blundevile for publication. At Gilbert's suggestion Briggs of Gresham College calculated out a table of dip and latitude. It was, however, soon found that the facts deviated more or less widely from the theory. Further observations in other lands showed the method to be impracticable; and Gilbert's hope to give to the mariner a magnetic measure of latitude remained unfulfilled. Book 5 closes with an eloquent passage in which Gilbert affirmed the neo-Platonic doctrine of the animate nature of the universe, and asserted that Thales was right when he held (as Aristotle relates in the *De Anima*) that the loadstone was animate, being part of and indeed the choice offspring of its animate mother the earth. Book 6, as already mentioned, is devoted to Copernican ideas, and contains Gilbert's one contribution to the science of Astronomy, in his remark that the fixed stars (previously regarded as fixed in the eighth of the celestial spheres at one common distance from the central earth) were in reality set in the heavens at various distances from the earth.

From this brief analysis it will be seen that Gilbert's claims to eminence rest not upon any particular discovery or invention, but upon his having built up a whole experimental magnetic philosophy on a truly scientific basis, in place of the vague and wild speculations which had previously been accepted. By his magnificent generalization from the small scale models to the globe itself, supported from point to point by experimental researches, he created the science of terrestrial magnetism. If from the imperfection of the data at his disposal he fell into sundry errors of detail, he yet founded the method of philosophizing by which those errors were in due time corrected. And if for nothing else than his masterly vindication of scientific method, and his rescue of the subject of magnetism from the pedantry and charlatanry into which in the preceding ages it had lapsed, his memory must be held in high honour.

Alas that of the personality of so great a man so little should be known. A brief but characteristic biography of him is enshrined by old Fuller in his *Worthies*. The poet Dryden, and the epigrammatist Owen, celebrated him in still briefer verse. His portrait, which hung for nigh two hundred years in the Schools Gallery, at Oxford, disappeared a century ago, leaving only a poor engraving to perpetuate his scholarly countenance. Doubtless he is one of the four physicians depicted by the pencil of Camden in his famous cartoon (now in the British Museum), as walking in the funeral procession of Queen Elizabeth. Of his handwriting not a vestige was known until about five years ago, when a signature was unearthed in the Record Office. Subsequently four signatures were found in the books of St. John's College; and recently there has come to light a volume of Aristotle bearing Gilbert's own marginal notes. His will lies at Somerset House, but it is only a copy. Of his fine collection of minerals and loadstones, which with his maps, books, manuscripts, and correspondence with Sarpi and Sagredo and others, he bequeathed to the College of Physicians, nothing remains: they perisht in the Great Fire of London. In a quiet corner of the City of Colchester stands the quaint old house where he lived, and where, according to local tradition, he once received the Queen. And hard by it is the church of Holy Trinity, in which a mural tablet records his virtues and marks his last resting place. But his true monument is the immortal treatise in which he laid the foundations of terrestrial magnetism and of the experimental science of electricity.

To the names of the men who made great the age of Queen Elizabeth, who added lustre to the England over which she ruled, and made it famous in foreign discovery, in sea-craft, in literature, in poetry, and in drama, must be joined that of the man who equally added lustre in science, Doctor William Gilbert.

This discourse on William Gilbert and terrestrial magnetism
in the time of Queen Elizabeth was delivered by Silvanus
P. Thompson at the meeting of the Royal Geographical
Society on March twenty-third MDCCCCIII on the
occasion of the tercentenary of the death of
Queen Elizabeth, and is now printed
by Charles Whittingham
and Company at the
Chiswick Press.